SPRINGER

The Rabbit Who Jumped Too High

Written by
Jeff Kallet

Illustrated by
Sarah Smith

Sometimes in this world of ours,
things happen that are weird,
but here's a goofy story
you may have never heard.

It's about a little rabbit—
a very special bunny—
who had a major problem
that for awhile wasn't funny.

SPRINGER'S
HOUSE

The problem with this rabbit
was never very clear—
he seemed to have a defect
in his jumping gear.

Perhaps it was a muscle,
it could have been a bone.
Maybe it was the vitamins
his mother had at home.

In any case, he jumped too high,
much higher than he liked,
and when he went to take a hop
he couldn't get it right.

Most rabbits hop a little,
they do their bouncing with some grace,
all except for Springer,
whose jumps could launch him into space.

From the pyramids of Egypt
to the ruins in Peru,
to Turkey, Greece and Singapore,
the little rabbit flew.

So helpless Springer sailed the skies,
not knowing where he'd go.
With just one hop, he'd fly to
France,
the next to Mexico.

Springer's dad took many trips
to find his wayward son;
"Springer's gone!" he'd tell his wife,
then off in search he'd run.

He'd find his son on peoples'
homes,
in cities and in rivers;
once they met at the North Pole,

There never was an answer
for what made Springer jump,
until the day he landed
in a distant city dump.

Sitting in a garbage heap
a hundred miles from home,
Springer met a wise old rat
who called himself the Gnome.

"Oh, Mr. Gnome I really wish
I wouldn't jump so far!"
Listening to the rabbit,
Gnome strummed on his guitar.

"I'm not sure what's causing this,"
sang the ancient rat,
"but if you want a magic cure,
I'll help you out with that."

Springer followed Gnome
past plastic, cans and rocks
until they came upon a bag
filled with old sweat socks.

"Try these on," sang the rat,
while pulling out a pair.
"I think you'll find they offer you
some guidance in the air."

The socks went way up past his ankles,
they went nearly to his tail,
but Gnome said not to worry,
"They have magic that won't fail."

"Now when you hop, just rub the socks,"
sang the rat to Springer.
"Rub from top to bottom,
and rub with every finger.

"And while you rub, just close your eyes
and let the magic happen;
anyplace you want to go,
you only need imagine."

Springer didn't understand,
he thought it was a trick,
but when he jumped into the air
the magic really clicked.

Rubbing up and down his legs,
Springer thought about his home
while flying through the atmosphere,
through three or four time zones.

Then he landed, nice and smooth,
now that was a surprise,
but a bigger one awaited him
when he opened up his eyes.

His mom and dad looked down at him,
they stared in disbelief.
"Son," they said, "this jumping thing
is causing lots of grief."

But that's when Springer pointed to
the socks upon his feet:
"Mom and Dad, don't worry,
I think I've got this beat.

"I met a rat, his name was Gnome,
I met him in a dump.
He gave these magic socks to me
which help control my jump.

"If I rub and concentrate
the jumping is a cinch;
with just a little mind control,
I can get home in a pinch."

"Son, I don't believe you,"
said Springer's father with some doubt,
"but let's go out into the woods
and try these sweat socks out."

So Springer told his parents
he'd be returning really soon,
and he told them both to keep their eyes
upon the light blue moon.

Then he took a jump that shot him up,
straight through the atmosphere.
"Holy moly!" said his dad;
his mother said, "Oh dear."

Rubbing with his fingers,
Springer flew right into space,
soaring past some meteors,
till moonlight touched his face.

After landing softly on the moon,
Springer did a little dance.
He hopped into a crater
and he wildly shook his hands.

One other thing that Springer did
to help secure his fame:
he bounced around the light
blue moon and spelled out
his own name!

In minutes Springer landed,
his fur blown in a fluff.
"Here I am, Mom and Dad,
was that done soon enough?"

His parents laughed, they jumped for joy,
and then they told their friends,
"Springer jumped up to the moon
and now he's back again!"

Springer became a hero,
among rabbits he was a star,
but he never failed to mention
the rat with a guitar.

He and Gnome became close friends,
they always kept in touch.
And Springer often told his pal,
"Thank you—very much!"